GRANT

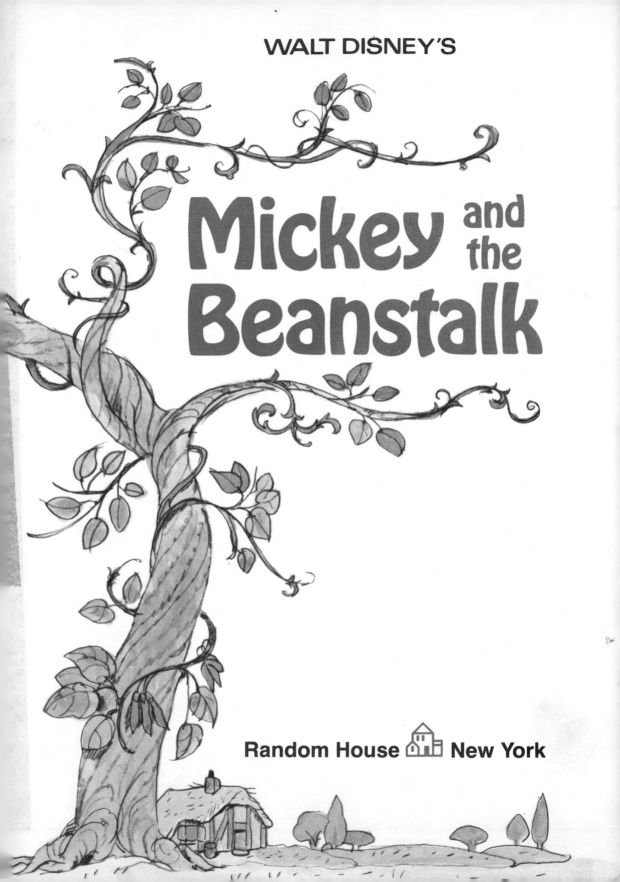

WALT DISNEY'S

Mickey and the Beanstalk

Random House New York

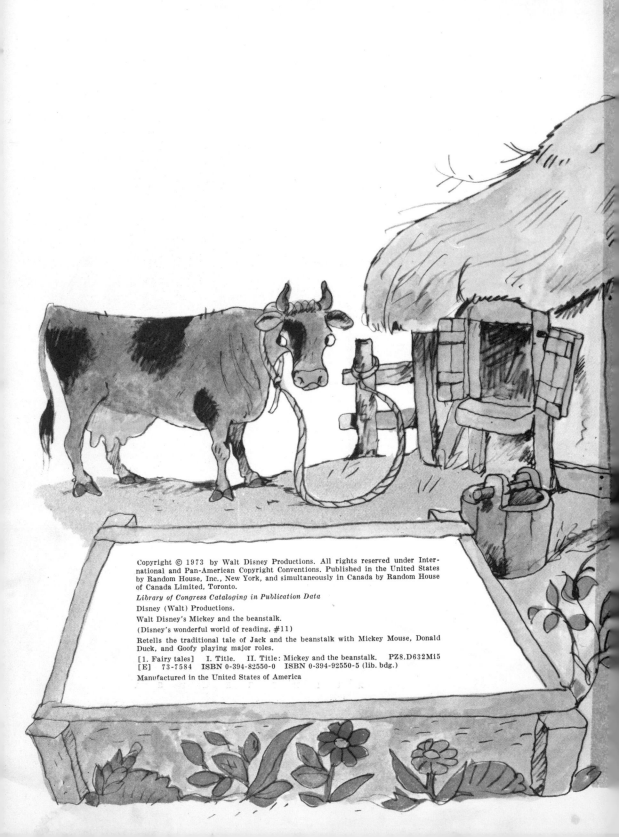

Copyright © 1973 by Walt Disney Productions. All rights reserved under Inter-
national and Pan-American Copyright Conventions. Published in the United States
by Random House, Inc., New York, and simultaneously in Canada by Random House
of Canada Limited, Toronto.
Library of Congress Cataloging in Publication Data
Disney (Walt) Productions.
Walt Disney's Mickey and the beanstalk.
(Disney's wonderful world of reading, #11)
Retells the traditional tale of Jack and the beanstalk with Mickey Mouse, Donald
Duck, and Goofy playing major roles.
[1. Fairy tales]   I. Title.   II. Title: Mickey and the beanstalk.   PZ8.D632Mi5
[E]   73-7584   ISBN 0-394-82550-0   ISBN 0-394-92550-5 (lib. bdg.)
Manufactured in the United States of America

A long time ago there were three friends
called Mickey, Donald, and Goofy.
They were very poor.
All they had was an old cow and a jar of beans.

One day there was just one bean left in the jar.
"We are down to our last bean," said Mickey.
"I hate beans!" said Donald.
"Beans are better than nothing," said Mickey.
"What do we eat now?" said Goofy. "I'm hungry."

Mickey looked out the window.

He saw the old cow.

"I know," said Mickey. "We can sell the cow."

So Mickey went off with the cow.

He was going to sell her

and buy some food.

"Remember!" called Donald. "No beans!"

On his way to town Mickey met an old woman.
"I'll trade you three beans for that cow!"
said the old woman.

"Beans for a cow!" cried Mickey. "Never!"

"These are not just just ANY beans,"
said the old woman. "They are magic beans!"

Now Mickey would never have traded the cow
for just any beans.

But magic beans were different.

So Mickey took them and gave her the cow.

When Mickey got back,
Donald and Goofy were all ready
to eat and eat and eat.
Mickey showed them the three beans.

"Beans!" cried Donald.

"But they are magic beans," said Mickey.

"I told you I hate beans," said Donald.

And he threw the beans out the window.

So Mickey, Donald, and Goofy had to go to bed
without any supper.

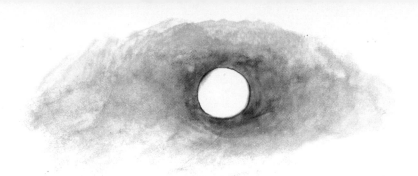

But the beans really WERE magic!

That night the moon found the first bean and it began to grow.

It grew and it grew and it grew—

right up into the sky!

When Mickey woke up,
he remembered the magic beans.
He ran to the window.
He saw a great beanstalk
growing right up into the sky!

Mickey decided to climb the beanstalk.

He climbed
    and he climbed
        and he climbed.

When he reached the top,
he saw a great big castle.

Mickey went into the castle.

He saw a great big table.

"A giant must live here," said Mickey.

On the table there was a great big cheese.
Mickey climbed up to take a bite.
Suddenly he heard a terrible sound.
THUMP! THUMP! THUMP!

The giant must be coming home!
Mickey hid in the cheese.
And just in time, too!
The giant had come home.
And he was feeling very hungry.

The giant began to sniff.
Then he said
in a low, mean voice:
"Fee-Fi-Fo-Fummee,
I smell a boy
And boys are yummy!
I'll roast that boy
And fill my tummy!"

The giant looked all around.
He looked in his sandwich.

He looked in his mug.
He was just about to look in his cheese . . .

Then he saw his bags of gold.
"Ah! My gold!" said the giant.
He liked his gold even more than he liked to eat.
So he decided to count it.

But soon the giant's head began to nod.
And soon the giant's eyes began to close.
And soon the giant began to snore.

Mickey jumped out of the cheese
and grabbed a bag of gold.

He ran to the beanstalk
and dropped the bag of gold.

Then he climbed down the beanstalk
as fast as he could go.

When Mickey reached the ground,
there were Donald and Goofy
catching the gold pieces.

"You won't believe this, Mickey," said Goofy.

"It's raining gold!" said Donald.

"No, it isn't," said Mickey.

"I found the gold at the top of this . . ."

But when he looked back, the beanstalk was gone!

That night the moon
found the second bean.
   And it began to grow, too.
   When Mickey woke up,
there was ANOTHER beanstalk.
   So he climbed it.

Mickey went inside the castle.

He hid in the oven.

And just in time, too!

THUMP! THUMP! THUMP!

The giant was coming home!

The giant was feeling very grumpy
about losing his bag of gold.
He began to sniff and say:
    "Fee-Fi-Fo-Fummee,
    I smell a boy
    And boys are yummy!
    I'll roast that boy
    And fill my tummy!"

The giant looked all around.
He looked in his stewing pot.

He looked in his teapot.
He was just about to look in his oven . . .

Then he saw his hen.
"My hen!" cried the giant.
The giant liked his hen
because it was a magic hen.
When the giant said, "Lay!"
the hen laid a golden egg.

Every time the giant said, "Lay!"
the hen laid still another golden egg.
But soon the giant's head began to nod.
And soon the giant's eyes began to close.
And soon the giant began to snore.

Mickey jumped out of the oven
and grabbed the hen.

He ran to the beanstalk
and dropped the hen.
Then he climbed
down the beanstalk
as fast as he could go.

When Mickey reached the ground,
he found Donald and Goofy looking at the hen.
"You won't believe this, Mickey," said Goofy.
"A hen fell out of the sky!" said Donald.
"No, it didn't," said Mickey.
"I found the hen at the top of this . . ."

But when he looked back,
the beanstalk was gone!

That night the moon found the third bean.
In the morning Mickey looked out the window.
And there was still ANOTHER beanstalk!
The magic had worked once more.
So Mickey climbed to the top.

He went inside the castle.
This time he hid in the fireplace.
And just in time, too!
THUMP! THUMP! THUMP!
The giant was coming home!

The giant was feeling very grumpy
about losing his hen that laid the golden eggs.
He sniffed and said:
"Fee-Fi-Fo-Fummee,
I smell a boy
And boys are yummy!
I'll roast that boy
And fill my tummy!"

The giant looked all around.
He looked in his wooden box.

He looked in his matchbox.

He was just about to look in his fireplace
when he saw his harp.
"My harp!" cried the giant.

Then the giant said, "Sing!"
And the harp began to sing a magic song.
She sang and she sang and she sang.

Soon the giant's head began to nod.
And soon the giant's eyes began to close.
BUT THE GIANT DID NOT SNORE!

Mickey jumped out of the fireplace.

He grabbed the harp and ran away.

He ran very fast.

But not fast enough!

The harp called out,

"Master! Master! Open your eyes!"

The giant opened his eyes

and saw Mickey running away with his harp.

The giant ran after Mickey.
But Mickey got to the beanstalk first.
He ran down as fast as he could go.
But the giant was right above him,
and he was getting closer and closer.

Mickey reached the ground first.
He grabbed an ax.
He chopped into the beanstalk
WHACK!
Down it came!
THUD!

That was the end of the giant!

From that day on,
the three friends were very happy.

Mickey traded the gold
for good things to eat.

Donald watched the hen
lay the golden eggs.

Goofy listened to the harp
play its magic song.

And they never ate beans again.